against the vegetable rack, using an onion as a ball. Dad had banned her from playing football in the garden, because she'd destroyed too many of his flowers and plants.

3

James was watching his favourite TV programme, *The Funky Show*, when a newsflash interrupted the show.

"INCREDIBLE NEWS JUST IN!" spluttered the presenter. "The entire Royal Family has decided to step down. They've had enough of being in the public eye and are fed up with talking to people they don't like."

"Unreal," whispered James.

"They'll be moving to Brighton in two weeks' time to set up a beachfront café," added the presenter. "It will be called 'Windsor Warmers' and will sell a wide variety of snack foods. We can now go live to the Chief Royal Advisor, Sir Cuthbert Snobbish, for more details."

The spindly body of Sir Cuthbert appeared on the screen, his long face looking solemn and serious.

"The Royal Family has insisted that a new king or queen must be chosen before they leave London," he said. "This will be done by way of a national competition, which the Royal Family will judge. The winner of this contest will be the person who..." Sir Cuthbert looked with disgust at the camera "... best completes the phrase 'I WANT TO BE KING/QUEEN OF ENGLAND BECAUSE...' in under fifteen words."

"No way!" James gasped.

"All entries must be in by next Saturday at midnight," continued Sir Cuthbert, shaking his head. "The result will be declared at three o'clock the following Sunday. After this announcement, the Royal Family will move out of Buckingham Palace and the competition winner and their family will move in."

A glint suddenly appeared in Sir Cuthbert's eyes. "However," he said, "if there are no entries or none of them are judged to be good enough, *I* will become King! This would be by far the best option, so I advise anyone thinking about entering the competition to forget it!"

James flicked the TV off and stood up quickly.

"I need a pen and piece of paper," he said.

By Sunday night, James had written 640 phrases for the Royal competition. The best three were:

I WANT TO BE KING OF ENGLAND BECAUSE...

I'd make the most delicious Royal sandwiches.

I'd close every school in the country, forever.

I'd invite my best mates to the Palace for a three-day food fight.

But none of them was good enough to win. He sighed deeply. He needed some serious help.

"Hold it still!" James hissed.

James was halfway up a ladder on the patio of Tabatha Crisp's garden. It was early evening on Tuesday. His best mates, Yaz and Dog, were at the bottom of the ladder trying to keep it steady. They'd both decided not to enter the competition but had agreed to help James.

Tabatha Crisp was the richest girl in James's class at Ridge Primary. Her house was known as Crisp Mansion. It had ten bedrooms, five bathrooms and an outdoor swimming pool. Tabatha had been boasting that she would win the Royal competition. She'd told everyone in their class that she'd hired the brilliant American Professor Von Tatler to write a winning phrase for her. He was emailing suggestions to her every day. When James had told Tabatha he was entering the competition, she'd laughed at him. "You're too scruffy to win," she said. "They'll choose someone with a bit of class and a brain – someone like me."

James finally reached Tabatha's open bedroom window.

The room was empty. A page entitled 'Winning Phrases To Make Tabatha Queen, by Professor Von Tatler', was flashing on her computer. If James could copy some of these and change them a tiny bit, he'd surely be in with a good chance of winning the competition. And even if he didn't win, he was determined to do better than Tabatha.

He slowly started pulling the window open.

It was then that the Crisp family's dog, Biter, started barking.

Yaz and Dog panicked as Biter stepped outside and onto the patio.

"Aaaaaahhh!" James yelled as the ladder tipped backwards and he flew into the Crisps' swimming pool, with a mighty splash.

Two seconds later Yaz and Dog dived into the pool to get away from Biter.

"What on earth's going on?" asked Mr Crisp, poking his head round the door and staring at the three drenched children in his swimming pool.

By Wednesday night, James still hadn't come up with a winning phrase. He'd managed to convince Tabatha's dad that he and his mates had been taking part in a charity window-cleaning marathon and had ended up in the pool for a wash after a hard day's work. But Tabatha hadn't believed him.

"Not only are you scruffy," she'd yelled, "but you're a cheat as well."

On Wednesday's evening news, Sir Cuthbert Snobbish was interviewed in the gardens of Buckingham Palace.

"It looks like there might not be a winner," he said with a fiendish glint in his eye. "If things stay this way, it means that reluctantly I will have to take on the role of King."

James noticed that Sir Cuthbert was wearing gloves and that his face looked hot and sweaty, even though it was a cold day.

"Interesting," murmured James.

On Thursday, during lunch break in school, James felt a tap on his shoulder. It was Tabatha Crisp.

"I know you were trying to steal Professor Von Tatler's ideas," she snarled.

"Go away, Tabatha," James replied irritably.

"When I become Queen," Tabatha continued, "I'm going to have a huge garden party for everyone I know. And if you're lucky, I'll employ you as a palace servant for the day."

"Dream on, Tabatha," said James, turning his back on her.

But James knew that time was running

out. If he didn't come up with something quickly, Tabatha's wish might just come true.

He wondered how much palace servants earned these days.

James held on to his remote-control helicopter tightly. It was four o'clock on Saturday afternoon. In just eight hours, the Royal competition would close. He was standing outside the gates of Buckingham Palace where he had persuaded Mum to bring him. (She had agreed reluctantly, on the understanding that she could sing her operatic favourites to passing tourists.)

James had strapped Dad's tiny video camera to the bottom of the helicopter. The pictures it took would be relayed to James on a small TV monitor he'd borrowed from Yaz. He looked around quickly to check where Mum was. She was waving her arms and singing to a young woman and her dog. The woman thought Mum was collecting for a charity dedicated to people who couldn't sing and threw a twenty pence coin at her feet.

The dog held its paws over its ears.

James directed the helicopter up in the air and over the high Palace walls.

The helicopter flew around to the back of the Palace and James checked his monitor carefully. Nothing. He flew the machine further. Still nothing. He cursed. Maybe his plan wouldn't work.

But just as he was about to bring the helicopter back, a wisp of smoke appeared at the corner of the screen. He flew the helicopter further forward and suddenly the person he'd been hoping to see came into view.

Sir Cuthbert Snobbish was tucked away in a remote corner of the Palace grounds, wearing gardening gloves and moving

around frantically, with a wild look in his eyes. James focused on him for a couple of minutes and then carefully steered the helicopter away. On no account must the Chief Royal Advisor see the flying craft.

James took the helicopter around the side of the palace. He increased its speed, watching on the monitor as it passed window after window. "Come on," whispered James to himself. "There must be someone inside." The helicopter was flying very fast now, flashing past windows as James became more desperate. Where was everyone?

And then he saw her.

At first she was just a blur as the helicopter sped past. But then he slowly pushed the reverse lever on the helicopter's remote-control panel. The helicopter flew backwards and James made it hover outside her window.

There she was!

It was one of the Princesses, peering out from behind a thick net curtain.

James flashed the warning light on the front of the helicopter.

For a few seconds nothing happened, and then the window was flung wide open. The Princess stared at the piece of paper that was stuck to the nose of the helicopter. Then she reached out her hand, grabbed it and slammed the window shut.

It all happened in a split second.

James allowed himself a smile and brought the helicopter back to his side. Mum was standing twenty feet away, singing in a screechy falsetto voice. Several tourists were running away from her and a baby in a buggy was crying (and making a more pleasant sound).

"Mum!" James called, "Let's go home."

The following Sunday afternoon, everyone in the country was tuned in to their TV, waiting for the competition announcement. James, Millwall, Mum and Dad were in the front room, glued to the screen.

At three o'clock exactly, the beaming face of Sir Cuthbert Snobbish appeared on screen.

"I am here to tell you..." he paused for dramatic effect "... that unfortunately *none* of the competition entries was quite good enough. So it is I who will now become—"

But before Sir Cuthbert could finish his sentence, a small figure appeared at his side and interrupted him. It was one of the Royal Princesses – the one who had taken the note from James's helicopter. She waved a piece of paper in the air for the nation to see.

"We only got this one," said the Princess, eyeing Sir Cuthbert with disgust, "but we all liked it. So we've sent Trevor to collect the winner."

Sir Cuthbert glared at the Princess in shock and fury.

"I think there's been some sort of mistake," he snarled, trying to snatch the letter from her hand. But the Princess jumped out of the way and said in her loudest voice, "And the winner is —"

But James and his family didn't get to hear the winner's name, because at that second there was a very loud knock on their front door.

Millwall ran to open it.

A smartly dressed chauffeur was standing outside wearing a dark suit and a grey cap. He handed Millwall a large purple envelope with a gold crown on the front.

Millwall took the envelope and slammed the door in his face.

The chauffeur pushed the letterbox flap open. "I'll be waiting in the car," he called.

The letter was addressed to Mr King. Millwall walked into the sitting room and threw the envelope at Dad.

He opened it and pulled out a cream piece of paper with silver lettering.

"What is it?" asked Mum.

"It seems I'm the winner of the Royal competition," said Dad.

"Hooray!" screamed Mum. "I can finally sing opera in the palace gardens!"

But Dad wasn't smiling. "It can't be right," he said.

"Why not?" spluttered Mum.

"Because I never entered."

James grinned and took the letter from Dad.

"I think that may be for me," he said trying to contain his excitement.

"Can't be," said Millwall. "It's addressed to 'Mr King'."

"Exactly," James nodded. "Mr *James* King."

He quickly scanned the letter.

"I'VE WON!" he cried. "I'VE WON, I'VE WON, I'VE WON!"

"Have you won?" asked Mum.

"We have to be at Buckingham Palace by six o'clock tonight!" screamed James, wild with excitement.

"I'M NOT COMING!" snarled Millwall, "There won't be any goalposts there."

"Who delivered the letter?" Dad asked.

"Some bloke with a cap." Millwall replied sulkily. He's waiting in a flash car."

"Get packing!" shouted James, running up to his bedroom, "WE'RE ON OUR WAY!"

20

James made sure Trevor drove the limousine past Crisp Mansion. Tabatha was standing outside on the pavement with twelve very expensive suitcases stacked up beside her. She stepped forward as the limo approached, expecting it to stop, but had to watch in dismay as it drove straight past her. James lowered his tinted window and gave her a regal wave.

The journey passed really quickly. Mum practised her scales, Dad potted a couple of plants he'd brought with him and Millwall tried doing headers with an armrest she'd ripped from one of the sleek, black leather seats.

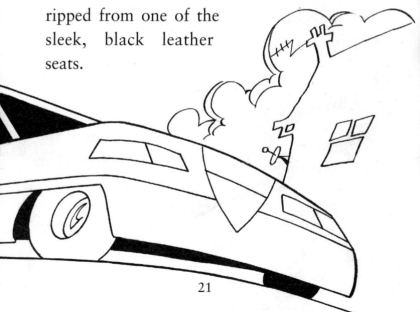

James sat back and just enjoyed the ride. As the car approached Buckingham Palace, the sound of clapping started up outside, getting gradually louder and louder. By the time the limo approached the golden Palace gates, there was a deafening noise of cheering and screaming. James lowered his window a fraction and the screams got wilder. There were thousands and thousands of people lining the streets, waving flags and cheering.

James gaped at the crowds in amazement as Trevor carefully steered the limo through the golden gates. As Trevor parked the limo, a multicoloured camper van pulled away. James could see every member of the Royal Family inside it.

"Have a look around" smiled Trevor, opening James's door first. "You've got a meeting with Sir Cuthbert in half an hour."

James and Millwall ran inside, with Mum and Dad walking behind them.

The Palace was truly gigantic.

"I reckon we could stick a couple of goalposts out here," James called to Millwall as he walked out onto the football-pitch-sized gardens.

"BRILLIANT!" screamed Millwall. She stepped forward to hug her brother.

However, immediately realising what she was doing, she turned the hug into a slap. Luckily James anticipated this and darted to the right, forcing her to smash a priceless Egyptian flowerpot.

Half an hour later, Sir Cuthbert Snobbish swept into the room.

"Right," he said with menace. "All you have to do is to wait here for a couple of hours until the crowds have gone away.

Then Trevor will drive you home and I can get on with being King."

"Thank you, but no thank you," smiled James.

"I BEG YOUR PARDON?" snarled Sir Cuthbert, towering over him.

"I think you'd better take a look at this," said James. "It might make you change your mind."

He slipped a DVD into a silver machine and turned on the giant plasma screen that covered one of the enormous walls.

The screen made a buzzing sound for a while, but no picture appeared.

"You are wasting everyone's time, pipsqueak!" shouted Sir Cuthbert. "You stay where you are, and when the fuss has died down you SCRAM!"

"But we're just getting to the good bit," winked James.

Suddenly the screen flickered into life.

"Take a little look at this," smiled James.

There on the screen, in full colour, was Sir Cuthbert Snobbish, standing in the Palace gardens in front of a colossal bonfire. He was whooping with delight, flailing his arms about and throwing hundreds of letters and postcards into the fire. The letters and postcards came from giant mail sacks, marked **'ROYAL COMPETITION ENTRIES'** in great big letters.

"NOOOOOO!" shrieked Sir Cuthbert, lunging for the DVD player.

"Take it if you like," James grinned, waving his hand theatrically in the air. "It's just that I made several copies and have sent them to the editors of every newspaper and television company in this country. If you don't play by the rules, the public gets to see your little performance. I don't think they'd take very kindly to it. Do you?"

Sir Cuthbert fell to his knees and burst out crying. "It should be me!" he wailed. "I want to be King!"

James looked down at Sir Cuthbert and cleared his throat. "I say we start as we mean to go on," he said firmly. "Everyone should know their place. Dad, you'll look after the

Palace gardens. Mum, you'll be in charge of music and parties. Millwall, you'll... you'll organise the Palace football team. And as for you, Sir Cuthbert – or shall I call you Cuthy? – I'm feeling a bit peckish..."

Sir Cuthbert stood up slowly and groaned.

"I'd like two plates of gherkin-and-chocolate-spread sandwiches," grinned James, "and a huge jug of lemonade, plus anything else my family wants."

"But... but... but..." stuttered Sir Cuthbert.

"Butter?" asked James. "Yes please, with some very large slices of bread."

Sir Cuthbert left the room, sobbing.

"So, what was your winning phrase?" grunted Millwall, planning to turn the ornate porcelain fireplace into a giant goal.

"I had a hunch that Sir Cuthbert was up to no good," said James. "I reckoned he was stopping all of the entries from getting through to the Royal Family. So I stuck mine to the front of my helicopter and got lucky. All I wrote was, 'I want to be King of England because... anyone would be better than Sir Cuthbert Snobbish, even a tin of baked beans!'"

"Nice one," nodded Millwall approvingly as she kicked her football against a tiny crystal sculpture and sent it flying out of a window.

"So yours was the only entry that made it?" gasped Mum in amazement, looking around the room and planning what to wear for her first operatic performance.

James nodded wisely.

"How do you feel now?" asked Dad, making a mental note of all the plants and flowers he'd need to order, to keep the grounds in tip-top shape.

James fell backwards onto a luxurious armchair, stretched his arms out and slowly took in his new surroundings.

"You know what?" he said with a smile, looking at his family. "I feel just like a king!"

JAMES
KING OF ENGLAND

and the Stolen Crown Jewels

The radio newsreader sounded very, very, very serious.

"Late last night, the world-famous Crown Jewels were stolen from the Tower of London," she said in a hushed voice. "There was no sign of a break in and the only people at the Tower were the Beefeaters. The sole key to the jewels case is on the key ring of the Chief Royal Advisor, Sir Cuthbert Snobbish, and he was at Buckingham Palace when the theft happened. The crime is a complete mystery."

Sir Cuthbert Snobbish switched off the radio. James, Millwall and Mum looked up at him.

Dad was far too busy to listen to the news. He was preparing his display for next week's Royal Garden Party.

"It's a national disaster," Sir Cuthbert snarled, looking at James, who was munching a carrot-and-lime-juice sandwich.

"To have the Crown Jewels stolen during your reign clearly shows that you are not fit to be King. You should leave the throne immediately!"

Before James could answer, there was a knock at the door and a man walked into the room. The only way to describe him would be 'hairy'. He had a long straggly beard, huge bushy eyebrows, thistles of hair sprouting out of his ears and whiskers jutting out of each nostril.

"May I present Inspector Bob Shins from Scotland Yard," Sir Cuthbert announced. "I have brought him here to solve the Case of the Crown Jewels ."

Inspector Shins stepped forward and stroked his long beard. "I have already conducted a thorough search of the Palace," he began, "and I found *this* in a silver lunchbox." He reached into his coat pocket and held up a shining gold sceptre, encrusted with diamonds.

"That's one of the Crown Jewels!" gasped Mum.

"Exactly!" cried Sir Cuthbert. "And that lunchbox belongs to K—"

"Actually it's mine," butted in Millwall. "Me and James swapped lunchboxes a couple of days ago."

"Aha!" declared the Inspector, "So Millwall is the thief!"

James, Millwall and Mum gaped at Shins with their mouths wide open.

"I'm sure you'll track down all the other jewels" hissed Sir Cuthbert.

"Of course I will," replied Inspector Shins, producing a huge bunch of jangling keys from another coat pocket. "But first it's off to the palace cells for you, Millwall. Then I'll continue my search."

"Great!" Millwall said, jumping off the sofa. "Do they have a Playstation down there?"

"Do we have to wear these masks?" moaned Yaz.

James, Yaz and Dog were stealthily climbing over the high walls of the Tower of London. It was late and the Tower was bathed in silvery moonlight.

"Of course!" whispered James. "I'm the King of England. One of the Beefeaters is sure to spot me."

James was wearing a sheep mask. Yaz had originally had a dog mask, but Dog wanted it. "It goes with my name," he'd insisted.

"Whatever," Yaz had replied. She was wearing a cheetah mask.

"Anyway, what are we doing here?" asked Dog, as they crept past a high wall.

"We're looking for clues, of course," James explained, "there's no way Millwall stole the jewels. They're all much too heavy for her to use as a football."

The three of them tiptoed along a gravel path and followed a sign that said, 'To the Crown Jewels'.

The door to the room was open and they crept inside. It was dark and gloomy.

"It's spooky," whispered Dog.

"I wonder if anyone came in here before their head was chopped off?" asked Yaz cheerfully.

"This way," mouthed James.

They walked to the far side of the room and there, standing before them, were the empty glass jewel cases, glinting in the moonlight.

"OK," said James, "let's split up. We need to look very carefully. Even the smallest clue could be useful."

The three of them began examining the cases, moving their fingertips slowly across the glass, searching for clues. After five minutes, they'd found nothing.

"Let's get out of here," said Dog.

"Yeah," nodded Yaz, "we did our best."

"Wait!" hissed James, reaching down to the floor and picking something up.

"What have you got?" asked Dog.

But at that second the lights suddenly came on and a large group of Beefeaters stormed into the room.

"We knew the thieves would come back!" one of them shouted.

"**GRAB THEM!**" yelled another.

James considered taking off his mask and showing the Beefeaters who he was. But they didn't look like they were in the mood for any explanations. So he just screamed,

"**RUN!**" at the top of his voice.

As the Beefeaters hurtled towards them, Yaz spotted a tiny door in the corner of the room. She grabbed its handle and yanked it open.

"This way!" she shouted.

She, James and Dog sped through the door, with the Beefeaters hot on their heels.

"Head for Tower Bridge!" James yelled.

"Bish them and bosh them!" a Beefeater called.

"Whack and thwack them!" another cried.

The children clambered over a wall. The Beefeaters may have been a bit older then them, but they were incredibly speedy.

"They're catching up!" screamed Yaz.

The Beefeaters were hopping down off the wall, only a few feet behind them. James and his friends hurtled down the road, but to their horror they saw both halves of Tower Bridge starting to rise. A huge boat was waiting to pass underneath it.

"FASTER!" yelled James.

The bridge was rising steadily – it looked like an impossible task. But the three of them were moving so fast that when they ran up their side of the bridge, the sheer speed carried them through the air to the other side in one swift move. They slid down onto the road below. The Beefeaters stood furiously on the other side of the bridge, shaking their fists and shouting.

The captain of the boat below saw a sheep, a dog and a cheetah scamper off down the road. "I must get some new glasses," he told himself.

Later that night the Royal Cook, Madame Bonjour, left the Palace kitchens and went outside to throw a rubbish sack into one of the giant Palace bins. As she opened the lid, she was greeted by a peculiar sight. Inside, covered in rubbish and holding up a grimy piece of paper, was James.

"Good evening, Madame Bonjour" he smiled, as if standing inside one of the Palace bins was completely normal.

"Good evening, Your Majesty," replied Madame Bonjour, as if finding the King standing inside one of the Palace bins was completely normal.

James climbed out of the bin. "I'd appreciate it if you didn't tell anyone about this little meeting," he said, as he walked past her back towards the Palace.

"Of course, Your Majesty" Madame Bonjour nodded, her eyes wide with surprise.

The next morning, James was in the Leisure Lounge sipping a frothy hot chocolate. Mum was sitting at a desk that was covered in envelopes.

"I've organised a special night of opera," she explained. "I'll be the star attraction. All of the ticket money will go into a special fund to buy some new Crown Jewels."

There was a huge pile of cash on the table. Mum was counting the money but hadn't bothered to read any of the letters. James picked up a letter.

Dear Mrs King

I enclose fifty pounds to pay you NOT to sing. I will send a further hundred pounds if you promise never to sing again,

Yours sincerely

Mr Albert Darlington

James picked up another one and then another. They were all written along the same lines. Each one begged Mrs King to keep her mouth firmly closed. He gathered all the letters together and stuffed them into his trouser pockets.

"I've made £8,500 so far," beamed Mum.

"The Great Music Hall will be totally full."

James poured himself another hot chocolate.

"Totally full," he agreed.

But by 'totally full', he meant 'totally empty'.

James left the Leisure Lounge and set off for the Palace gardens. It was Yaz's birthday and he'd planned a big surprise for her.

When Yaz arrived everything was in place. James made Yaz close her eyes as he and Dog led her into the gardens.

"Open them!" said James.

"Unreal!" laughed Yaz after opening her eyes.

There on the lawn was an enormous hot-air balloon, with a pilot in a blue jumpsuit and flying goggles.

"I discovered there's a Royal Balloon," James grinned, "and I thought a trip in it would make a slightly better present than a book token."

James, Yaz and Dog ran towards the balloon and the pilot helped them climb into the basket. The pilot pulled a cord and the balloon lifted gracefully into the sky. A minute later it was gliding through the air. Yaz pulled out the present from her parents – a large pair of binoculars.

"I can see your dad," she laughed, looking down at the Palace gardens. "He's singing to some roses. And behind the garden that's... oh... that's... it's..."

"It's what?" butted in James, grabbing the binoculars. He could just make out a pair of hands digging in the Palace gardens, right in the middle of a patch of Dad's favourite daffodils. The rest of the person was hidden behind a thick oak tree. Then James saw a flash of red and gold. But he didn't see it for long because Dog grabbed the binoculars to look for himself. Yaz then grabbed them back. James quickly grabbed them again. By this point the pilot was feeling a bit left out, so he grabbed them. As he was trying to focus them, the hot-air balloon suddenly collided with a particularly large tree.

" AAAAHHHHHHHHHHHHHH!
everyone screamed.

That night James was standing outside the Palace cells, looking at his sister through the iron bars. He had just explained how he, his mates and the pilot had escaped from the Royal Balloon by jumping out and landing on a giant bouncy castle, which was being tested by Palace Staff in preparation for the Royal Garden Party.

"What about you?" James asked Millwall. "How's life in the cells?"

"It's great!" she grinned. "Really damp and filthy."

She suddenly frowned.

"What is it?" said James. "Aren't they feeding you properly?"

"No, the food's fine," Millwall sighed, "but there isn't a TV. And, worse still, there's no one to play football with. I found an old skeleton but it didn't even want to have a simple kick-about."

"I'll see what I can do about a match," James promised, "but first I'll make sure you get a decent telly."

James left the cells and headed for the Great Music Hall. When he got there, the lights were all off. He was about to flick them on when he saw a shadowy figure hurrying out through another door. Even though it was pretty dark, James could see something thin and orange sticking out of the figure's top jacket pocket.

"Strange," mused James to himself. He decided to leave piano playing for another time and strode away from the hall.

"Is that enough?" asked Dog.

"No, one more," answered James.

It was an hour before breakfast. James, Yaz and Dog had got up early to prepare for the risky task ahead.

"Ok" James nodded, "I'm going in."

Yaz silently pulled open the door. James got down on his hands and knees and started crawling across the spotless blue-and-white lino. Madame Bonjour wouldn't tolerate anyone other than her chefs entering her sacred Palace kitchens. There was a tiny glass panel in the door and Yaz put her eye against it.

James edged his way across the lino. He couldn't move quite as fast as he wanted, but he was making good progress. When he was halfway across, a pan suddenly clattered onto a surface somewhere behind him. The noise startled him and he slipped, nudging a trolley. The trolley rolled forwards and crashed into the knees of the pancake chef. This made the pancake chef throw a pancake wildly across the kitchen, where it landed on the head of the soup chef.

"How's it going?" asked Dog. Yaz was watching through a tiny window.

"Pretty bad," replied Yaz.

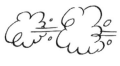

The soup chef screamed
as the pancake hit him
and he leapt
backwards into
a huge tureen
of cold soup,
splashing large
splodges of
pea soup on
the pastry
chef's pastries.

"How's it
looking?" asked
Dog.

"Worse," replied Yaz.

"YOU IDIOT!" screamed the pastry chef
at the soup chef.

"How's it looking?" asked Dog.

"Don't ask," replied Yaz.

A couple of seconds later Madame
Bonjour turned around and saw what had
happened to her pancake, soup and pastry
chefs. She let out a blood-curdling scream.

As all the other chefs turned to look at her,

James quickly scuttled across the last few inches of lino.

He'd made it.

As darkness fell that evening, James crept out into the garden. Dad was in a greenhouse arguing with a pot plant.

"Psst! Dad!"

Dad looked up. James beckoned Dad over and handed him a large cardboard box. "There's loads of stuff in here for your garden display," whispered James.

"Thanks," replied Dad. "Why are we whispering?"

"We're not," whispered James.

"OK," whispered Dad.

Dad opened the box and James slunk out, making straight for the Leisure Lounge. His favourite TV quiz show, *Word Wizard*, was just starting. He bit into a tuna-and-maple-syrup pancake and tried to concentrate on the programme. But half his mind was elsewhere. He was going over the theft of the

Crown Jewels in his head and something just wasn't fitting into place. He was about to flick off the telly to think a bit harder, when the presenter announced that it was time for the bonus round. As the letters flashed across the screen, James suddenly sat bolt upright.

"First of all, I want to thank everyone for being here," said James. It was nearly midnight and the sky was a bluey black.

He was standing in the Palace gardens with Dad, Mum, Sir Cuthbert and Inspector Shins. In the Palace cells Millwall was watching a live link-up on the plasma-screen TV James had ordered for her.

"Can you get on with it?" moaned Shins. "I've still got the rest of the jewels to find."

"Sure," smiled James. He flicked a switch and everyone was dazzled by a flash of brilliant white light. When their eyes adjusted, they saw in front of them the most incredible garden display. Included in the display was every single one of the missing

Crown Jewels. Each jewel had a plant sticking out of it or a flower wrapped around it.

"What the...?" gasped Inspector Shins.

"How the...?" gasped Sir Cuthbert.

James turned to face them. "Let me explain," he began. "As soon as Inspector Shins found the sceptre in Millwall's

lunchbox, I was suspicious. Millwall only has time for one thing. If you gave her a million pounds she'd only try to fold the notes and make them into a football. There's no way she'd steal even one Crown Jewel. So I began my own investigation. I started at the Tower and I found a torn piece of paper by the empty display cases. Rooting around in the Palace bins later, I found the other half of that paper."

"Clever you!" mocked Sir Cuthbert.

James ignored him and continued. "Then when I was up in the Royal Balloon, I spied a pair of hands digging and burying something red and gold in the Palace gardens."

"So that's why my daffodils were trampled down!" huffed Dad.

"Next," James said, "I saw a shadowy figure leaving the Great Music Hall with a frozen fish finger jutting out of their top jacket pocket."

"Frozen fish finger?" snorted Inspector Shins. "This sounds like nonsense to me!"

"It's preposterous!" shouted Sir Cuthbert. "It's monstrous. It's ridiculous."

He tried to think of another word ending in 'ous', but couldn't.

"OK, clever clogs," sneered Inspector Shins. "If you know so much, who is the thief?"

"Well," smiled James, "The thief is..."

He paused for a few seconds... "... Sir Cuthbert Snobbish!"

"How dare you?" screamed Sir Cuthbert, holding his chest.

"Everyone knows I was at the Palace on the night of the crime!"

"Of course you were," smiled James, "but you got your accomplice to do the dirty work."

"Accomplice?" asked Mum and Dad at the same time.

"Yes" nodded James. "You see, the piece of paper I found was from a key-cutting shop. Sir Cuthbert made a copy of the key and gave it to his partner in crime. The pair of hands I saw from the balloon were Sir Cuthbert's. I recognised the ring on his left hand. He was burying a red-and-gold Beefeater's tunic. His accomplice dressed up as a Beefeater to gain entry to the Tower. Cuthy was burying the evidence."

"This is ludicrous!" yelled Sir Cuthbert, suddenly remembering another word ending in 'ous.'

"It was Sir Cuthbert hurrying out of the Great Music Hall. The frozen fish finger in his jacket indicated that he'd been somewhere very, very cold that stores food. So Yaz and Dog helped me dress in fantastically warm clothes and I crept through the kitchens and entered the massive walk-in freezer. After a quick search, I found a box containing the Crown Jewels. They'd been stashed there because it was one of the least obvious hiding places in the Palace. I grabbed the box and gave it to Dad for his garden display."

"Very kind of you," said Dad.

"It seems clear now that Sir Cuthbert was behind the theft," whispered Mum. "But who on earth was his accomplice?"

James suddenly lunged forward and pulled at Inspector Shins's beard, eyebrows, ear thistles and nose whiskers. They all came off in his hands.

"Underneath all that hair, Inspector Shins looks very much like Sir Cuthbert!" Mum gasped.

"Precisely," beamed James. "I'd worked most things out but there was still a vital missing link. When I was watching *Word Wizard* on TV, the penny finally dropped. 'Bob Shins' is an anagram of 'Snobbish'. Shins is really Sir Cuthbert's younger brother, Sir Herbert Snobbish. They cooked up the

Crown-Jewels robbery to embarrass me in an attempt to get me off the throne. They planted the sceptre in what they thought was my lunchbox, but of course is now Millwall's."

Sir Cuthbert and Sir Herbert both let out shrieks of protest and started to hit each other.

"It's your fault, Cuthbert," wailed Herbert.

"It's your fault, Herbert," screamed Cuthbert.

"You can argue it out in the Palace cells," declared James, producing a bunch of jangly keys and leading the livid brothers away.

As James ushered Sir Cuthbert and Sir Herbert into the cell he beckoned for Millwall to come out.

"Aaaawwww!" she complained. "I wanted to see what happened to my hair if I didn't wash it for a year."

"You can still do that." James pointed out. "Anyway, you wouldn't want to miss the five-a-side football tournament I've organised for the Royal Garden Party would you?"

"NO WAY!" screamed Millwall, jumping up to hug her brother. However, immediately realising what she was doing, she turned the hug into a slap. Luckily James anticipated this and darted backwards, forcing her to knock over Sir Cuthbert and Sir Herbert.

Later that night, James, Yaz and Dog sat on the balcony, looking out onto the Palace lawns. Dad was scurrying about, putting the finishing touches to his garden display.

The three of them were silent for a moment, enjoying the warm night air.

"Having helped me to solve the Crown-Jewels case, do you know what you two are?" asked James suddenly.

Yaz and Dog shook their heads.

James looked at them and laughed.

"You're complete diamonds!"

JAMES
KING OF ENGLAND

and the New National Anthem

James King reached for one of the cheese-and-blueberry sandwiches that the Royal Cook, Madame Bonjour, had prepared for him. He was just about to tuck in, when there was a loud knock on his bedroom door. The tall, spindly figure of Chief Royal Advisor, Sir Cuthbert Snobbish, slithered into the room.

"You called?" hissed Sir Cuthbert.

"Yes, Cuthy," smiled James. (Sir Cuthbert hated nothing more than being called 'Cuthy'). "When the crowd at the art-gallery opening sung the National Anthem this morning, they sounded like a bunch of moaning sheep."

"And?" asked Sir Cuthbert.

"And I've decided it's time for a change."

"You mean – get a professional choir to sing it?" nodded Sir Cuthbert solemnly.

"No, Cuthy. What we need is a completely *new* national anthem – something modern and funky, like songs by The Groove Police."

Sir Cuthbert's cheeks blushed crimson and he had a violent coughing fit. When he'd finished, he held up a finger in protest.

"I'm afraid I can't allow The Groove Police or any other pop band anywhere *near* the National Anthem. It's been a central part of this country for many, many years and it **CANNOT** be changed, not by you or anyone else."

"Thanks, Cuthy," James nodded. "I see your point."

Sir Cuthbert smiled smugly.

"But I'm going to ignore it," added James. "The search for a new anthem will begin today!"

"A bit more to the left!" Yaz called.

James and his best mates, Yaz and Dog, were leaning over one of the Palace balconies, trying to hang a huge banner across the front of the Palace.

"Up a bit," said Dog. "Get it level with the top of the balcony."

They all pulled at the huge piece of canvas.

"Your bit's not straight," James said to Dog.

Dog leaned even further forwards and toppled over the edge of the balcony."

AAHHHH!" he yelled.

Quick as a flash, James leapt towards Dog and grabbed his ankles.

"AAHHHH!"

yelled Dog again as he hung upside down, swinging against the side of the Palace, 200 feet above the tiny cars in the street below.

"Stick it there!" yelled James.

"What are you talking about?" shouted

Dog, "JUST GET ME OUT OF HERE!"

"We will!" said James. "But since you're down there, you might as well sort out that last corner."

Dog sighed and tried not to look down again. He reached out for the piece of canvas and stuck it into place.

"Are you happy now?" he yelled up at James and Yaz.

"Excellent work!" grinned James as he and Yaz pulled Dog back up and over the balcony to safety. The three of them carefully looked down at the huge banner.

ANTHEM QUEST
ARE YOU A BUDDING COMPOSER?

Could you write a new national song?
Would you like your tune sung
at football matches?

Then ANTHEM QUEST is for you!!!
All entries welcome

TOP FIVE ANTHEMS will go into a live,
televised grand final

Within an hour of the banner going up, everyone in the country knew about ANTHEM QUEST. People who had never even thought about composing music before suddenly became song writers.

By early evening, a giant queue had formed outside the Palace, snaking for miles into the distance. There were people playing drums, practising on violins and scribbling musical notes on the back of empty crisp packets. There were even two eighty year-old sisters pushing a grand piano while humming out new tunes to each other.

"But you're my son!"

James was playing Daredevil Racers on the huge computer screen in the Palace's Leisure Lounge. He always liked to have a game before he went to bed.

He pressed 'pause' and turned to face his mother. She was wearing a flowing, jewel-encrusted dress with a red rose in her hair.

"There's no need for a contest to find a new anthem, James," she announced. "I've already written one – and I am, after all, a world-famous opera singer."

James's mum was not world famous, nor could she sing, but he didn't think it was a good time to mention these facts. Instead he said, "All rright Mum, let's hear it."

Mum stepped back, took a deep breath and opened her mouth. What followed was less of a song and more of a cross between a shriek and a piercing scream. Within five seconds every mirror in the room had cracked.

At that moment, Sir Cuthbert appeared in the doorway. His hands were clamped over his ears to block out the ear-splitting sound. He strode towards Mum and slipped on the TV remote control that was lying on the floor. Suddenly the TV flickered into life and there, on the screen appeared ace reporter Bella Compton. She was standing beside the ever-lengthening queue outside the Palace.

Mum suddenly stopped 'singing.' She, James and Sir Cuthbert gazed at the screen.

"Everyone here is camping overnight so that they don't lose their place in the queue," said Bella. "I've spent the last half hour asking different people why they're taking part in ANTHEM QUEST."

"I want to be on a stamp," squeaked a small boy.

"Every time the anthem is played, I'll get paid," remarked a teenage girl.

"I'm looking for my cello teacher," explained a man with a very long moustache.

"Isn't this the table-tennis tournament?" asked a young woman in a tracksuit.

James picked up the remote control and turned the TV off.

Mum stared around the room at the broken mirrors. "On second thoughts," she said, "maybe ANTHEM QUEST isn't for me. Perhaps I'm just too *good*."

"Exactly," nodded James with relief.

Sir Cuthbert suddenly smiled very broadly.

"What are you so happy about all of a sudden, Cuthy?" James asked.

"I just enjoy serving you, Your Majesty" replied Sir Cuthbert as his ears wiggled. (Sir Cuthbert's ears always wiggled when he was lying.)

James was too tired to ask Sir Cuthbert any other questions. "Let's all get some sleep," he yawned. "Tomorrow's a massive day."

The next morning's newspapers all had front-page stories about ANTHEM QUEST.

"How very exciting," Sir Cuthbert grinned at breakfast, pointing out the newspaper headlines while passing James his peanut-and-lettuce sandwiches. "It's going to be a wonderful contest."

James looked up suspiciously. "Hang on a second, Cuthy. I thought you were totally against the idea of ANTHEM QUEST."

Sir Cuthbert smiled his most sickly-sweet smile. "Perhaps I was wrong, Your Majesty. Maybe it is time for a change."

Sir Cuthbert backed out of the room, making little bows. Just before he disappeared from view, James spied something poking out of his briefcase.

"Fascinating," James muttered to himself.

At nine o'clock Madame Bonjour flung open the gigantic, golden Palace gates and the great queue of people started slowly moving forward.

There was a panel of two judges for ANTHEM QUEST – James and Millwall. They sat behind a large oak desk at the far side of the Great Music Hall.

James knew that every pop contest had to have a horrible judge and Millwall had gladly volunteered for this role, in return for James promising her he'd arrange a football match after the final.

Each contestant would have the chance to perform their song. But if James or Millwall thought the song was rubbish, Millwall got to kick her football at the contestant as hard as possible. That meant they were out.

James and Millwall had to choose the five best entries. These five lucky contestants would go into the live, grand final in forty-eight hours. However, to keep the level of excitement sky high, the identities of these five finalists would remain a total secret until the final.

The first contestant, a young girl carrying a recorder, walked nervously across the hall.

"OK!" beamed James. "Let's hear what you've got for us!"

By that evening, James and Millwall had spent twelve hours in the Great Music Hall. Thousands of contestants had been knocked over by Millwall's ball and had left the Palace with nothing (apart from a few bruises). Of those contestants who'd stayed standing, some had lasted as long as a minute, whereas others had been 'rung off' by James's bell after a few seconds.

After much discussion, James and Millwall had selected their five favourite entries. These five finalists had been whisked away to a hotel in a secret location, far away from the prying eyes of the press and the public.

"CHECK THIS OUT!" shouted Yaz.

She leapt into the air and landed back on her surfboard.

James, Yaz and Dog, were surfing on the gigantic waves that the Palace wave machine was making on the surface of the Palace swimming pool.

As they jumped off their surfboards and climbed out of the pool, a sound caught James's attention.

"What is it?" asked Dog and Yaz together.

James beckoned them forward with one finger and they followed him silently down by the side of the pool and out into a narrow passageway. As they crept forward the noise got louder until James stopped completely.

They all listened for a minute.

"Are you thinking what I'm thinking?" James whispered.

Yaz and Dog looked back at him.

Then they both nodded.

There was a buzz of feverish whispering as the excited audience fidgeted in anticipation. The camera operators checked their lenses and moved stealthily across the floor. Suddenly the studio lights went down and a single spotlight picked out a circle on the centre of the stage.

"Ladies and gentlemen," boomed a voice. "Welcome to Silver Town Studios for tonight's live and televised grand final of ANTHEM QUEST! Please put your hands together for your Royal host, James King of England!"

There was thunderous applause and cheering as James stepped inside the circle of light.

"Good evening," he smiled "and welcome to ANTHEM QUEST."

There was more clapping and whistling.

"Thousands and thousands of people entered this contest," James said. "And it was very close. But five anthems have been chosen and tonight it's my privilege to reveal the identities of the five performers."

"TELL US! TELL US! TELL US!" chanted the audience.

"Ladies and
gentlemen," James
continued, "our
first ANTHEM
QUEST finalist is
the delightful,
Tara Foxtrot!"

Tara leapt onto the
stage, wearing a tight blue dress, enormous
silver hoop earrings, and shoes with twenty-
five-inch heels. She began a high-tempo
dance routine and started singing her
anthem, *Buckingham Boogie*. She oozed with
confidence as she strutted around the stage
with an enormous smile on her
face, revealing her
gleaming white teeth.
The audience lapped
it up – it was a near-
perfect performance.

But during a very
complicated jump-
and-twirl move, Tara
caught one of her heels

on a loose floorboard. She swayed for a few seconds as the audience gasped in shock. For a moment it seemed as if she'd got her balance back but the next thing everyone saw was Tara toppling over and falling headfirst through a trap door in the centre of the stage.

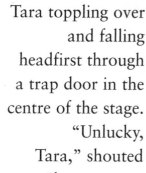

"Unlucky, Tara," shouted James, "but we must move straight on. Next up is the soulful Steve Peeve."

Back at the Palace, Steve had been brilliant. He'd tenderly plucked his Spanish guitar and sung his anthem, *Mad about the Monarch*, with soul and passion. He started in the same style, looking fantastic in his tight

black suit, beanie hat and shiny brown boots. Everyone in the audience hummed along with his sweet tune. But during the second chorus, when extra spotlights were trained on his face, Steve was suddenly overcome by the tension and excitement of the event. He tried to carry on with his song but, instead of *singing* into the microphone, he *bit* it and yelped with pain.

"Bad luck!" yelled James, throwing a card with the phone number of the Royal Dentist at Steve, who ran off the stage clutching his mouth.

"Two down, three to go," James informed the audience. "Third up we have the multi-talented Miss Angela Lamplight."

Angela used an overhead rope to swing onto the stage. She was wearing combat trousers, a green t-shirt and heavy-duty army boots. Thunderous beats roared out of the speakers at the side of the stage and Angela began her brilliant rap, *Big It Up for the Throne*. People in the audience thumped their feet on the floor in appreciation and rocked their bodies in time with the rhythm. When Angela was halfway through the rap, it seemed she might be well on the way to winning ANTHEM QUEST. But for no apparent reason, she forgot the rest of her words and began to rap the words of *The Grand Old Duke of York* instead.

"Better luck next time, Angela," James shouted, ushering a bewildered Angela off the stage. "So, ladies and gentlemen, our first three contestants are all out of the competition. That leaves us with a showdown between our last two contestants."

"Who are they? Who are they? Who are they?" yelled the audience with manic, nervous energy.

James looked out at the sea of faces. "I can now reveal that the first of these two showdown contestants is... Mr Elvis Fish-Horn, with *A Song to Sing for a Super Cool King.*"

The crowd went wild, screeching at the tops of their voices and clapping until their hands were sore. Elvis bounded on to the stage in his white cape, glittery red trousers, enormous sunglasses and massively gelled hair. He grabbed the mic, started singing feverishly and dived across the stage – skidding forward on his knees. He wiggled his hips. He threw the microphone in the air. He curled his upper lip. The audience cheered wildly and clapped along with him.

Elvis was so excited by the audience's response that he reached forward into the front row and grabbed the outstretched hand of a screaming young woman. He pulled her up onto the stage and she beamed with joy and waved to the TV cameras. Elvis flung her around the stage and flicked her over his shoulder.

People yelled even louder, so Elvis flung the woman high into the air. He was so busy gyrating for the audience that he didn't see her come crashing back down to earth. She landed on him with a huge thump. Elvis was knocked out and lay motionless on the floor. The young woman was fine and she ran over to help him, but Millwall quickly rushed onto the stage, pushed the young woman back into her seat and dragged Elvis off by his feet.

There was pandemonium in the TV studio. There was only one contestant left! People were jumping on their seats, slapping each other with anticipation and braying like farmyard animals.

James managed to calm the audience down for a few moments. "We are now down to our very last finalist," he announced. "As long as they get through their piece, they will be the winner of ANTHEM QUEST and take their place in history. So it is my pleasure to tell you that the last contestant is…"

He paused dramatically as the audience held their breath.

"… The one and only Carla Candy!"

The audience went completely berserk. Several people climbed up the safety curtain, screaming. One young man performed a mid-air double somersault, even though he normally couldn't do a simple forward roll.

"Tonight," boomed James, "for your delight, Carla will be performing her very own anthem, *Rock the Palace*!"

The audience whistled, cried and barked.

Carla ran onto the stage, barely able to contain her excitement. She swished the long pink shawl draped around her shoulders. She fluttered her extra-long eyelashes. She slanted her purple floppy hat at an angle. She twirled the ringlets of her long blonde hair. Then she began to sing in her unique, squeaky, high voice. The studio was filled with deafening clapping, cheering and chanting, as Carla grinned delightedly and glided across the stage.

She was well into *Rock the Palace*, when suddenly there was a very loud noise from the backstage area. Almost immediately, an enormous gust of wind swept across the stage.

Carla tried to carry on singing, but it was impossible. She desperately hung onto her pink shawl, but a second later it blew off her shoulders. Her enormous false eyelashes left her face and whooshed across the stage. As the powerful wind blew, Carla's purple hat started swaying. She grabbed it, but it was too late. It had sped off too. Finally her hair started flying about. She snatched at her golden ringlets, trying to keep them under control. But it was no good. The ringlets danced in all directions and then flew right off her head and landed on a sleeping child in row seventeen of the Dress Circle.

It was a wig!

And underneath the wig Carla was completely bald.

And the bald person was really a man.

The studio audience burst into hysterical laughter.

"What a surprise!" beamed James from the side of the stage, as he switched off the giant fan that was used to create wind effects for TV shows.

"Ladies and gentlemen" he shouted. "My Chief Royal Advisor – Sir Cuthbert Snobbish!"

Sir Cuthbert tried to step away from the giant spotlight, but it followed him wherever he went.

"How did you know I was Carla Candy?" he shrieked.

James grinned. "When you heard someone on TV say they'd be paid every time their anthem was played, I noticed you suddenly got interested in ANTHEM QUEST. Then, when I spotted a purple hat hanging out of your briefcase, my suspicions grew. And finally, when I was down in the swimming pool with Yaz and Dog, I heard you singing *Rock the Palace* in one of the showers. Suddenly I knew what you were up to!"

Sir Cuthbert shook his fists in the air. "Carla will be back!" he yelled. Then he ran off the stage, colliding with a man holding a large tray of choc-ices. James's mum leapt onto him and started wiping the chocolate marks off his head.

"Anyway." James laughed, turning to the audience, "I've decided the old anthem isn't that bad after all. It just needs a bit of jazzing up."

He clicked his fingers and suddenly the five members of The Groove Police ran onto the stage and started performing the most incredible version of the National Anthem. The entire studio audience jumped to their feet and began dancing crazily.

James leaned over to Millwall. "You'll be pleased to know that I've chosen two sides from the audience and arranged a football match for you," he whispered. "Kick off's after the show in the car park."

"AMAZING!" screamed Millwall stepping forward to hug her brother. However, immediately realising what she was doing, she turned the hug into a slap. Luckily James anticipated this and darted to the right. Unluckily this forced her to knock a lighting technician off his ladder and onto the shoulders of an elderly woman dancing in the aisle.

James noticed Dad at the side of the stage, taking cuttings from a rose bush and talking to it. He looked up when James came across towards him.

"I've ordered some new petunias from the garden centre," Dad said. "Oh, and Madame Bonjour phoned to say she's made you some dandelion-and-butterscotch sandwiches for your return to the Palace tonight. She wanted to know if that was OK?"

"It's more than OK," James winked. "It's music to my ears!"

Professor Mudgett and his daughter, Sally, live in a little house in a rubbish dump and dream of better things.

When one of the professor's 'secret formulas' goes wrong, Sally throws it into the garden and strange things begin to happen. Enter the world of Sally Mudgett and meet the wacky professor, the blue dragon and an evil restaurant owner who likes to be called The Mighty King Poe!

£3.99 1-84539-100-4

OTHER FANTASTIC FICTION FROM

meadowside
CHILDREN'S BOOKS

Follow the master of menacing through a maze of mischief and mayhem.

£3.99 1-84539-098-9

Grown-ups and softies beware – Dennis is on a mission to menace!

£3.99 1-84539-095-4

OTHER FANTASTIC FICTION FROM

meadowside
CHILDREN'S BOOKS

Everyone knows a menace
somewhere...
Now read about the
greatest menace ever!

£3.99 1-84539-097-0

Dennis is back! Join the
mighty menace
as he creates more crazy
chaos!

£3.99 1-84539-096-2

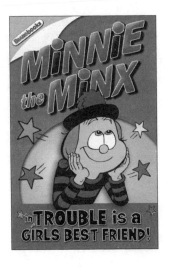

MORE FANTASTIC FICTION COMING FROM

meadowside
CHILDREN'S BOOKS

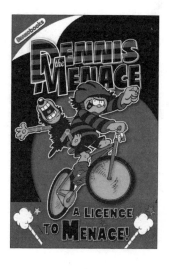

£3.99 1-84539-204-3

£3.99 1-84539-205-1

What will The Beano's famous bad boy do next?

Find out in these three entertaining new Dennis the Menace stories, and follow the master of menacing through a maze of mischief and mayhem.

For Jake and Ben
J.Z.

For Eileen.
B.A.

First published in 2006
by Meadowside Children's Books
185 Fleet Street, London, EC4A 2HS

Text © Johny Zucker 2006
Illustrations © Barrie Appleby 2006
The rights of Johny Zucker and Barrie Appleby to be identified
as the author and illustrator of this work have been asserted
by them in accordance with the Copyright,
Designs and Patents Act, 1988

A CIP catalogue record for this book
is available from the British Library
Printed and bound in England by William Clowes Ltd, Beccles, Suffolk

10 9 8 7 6 5 4 3 2 1

ISBN 1-84539-101-2
ISBN 978-1-84539-101-X